C c   D d   E e

I i   J j   K k

N n   O o   P p

T t   U u

X x   Y y   Z z

BEATRICE

Spells Some Lulus and Learns to Write a Letter

Cari Best

Pictures by
Giselle Potter

MARGARET FERGUSON BOOKS
Farrar Straus Giroux
New York

For spelling Beas
and their grandmas,
and for
Thomas Jefferson, too
—C.B.

For Pia and Isabel
and their creative spelling
—G.P.

Farrar Straus Giroux Books for Young Readers
175 Fifth Avenue, New York 10010

Text copyright © 2013 by Cari Best
Pictures copyright © 2013 by Giselle Potter
All rights reserved
Color separations by Embassy Graphics Ltd.
Printed in China by Macmillan Production (Asia) Ltd.,
Kowloon Bay, Hong Kong, (supplier code 10)
Designed by Roberta Pressel
First edition, 2013
1 3 5 7 9 10 8 6 4 2

mackids.com

Library of Congress Cataloging-in-Publication Data
Best, Cari.
  Beatrice spells some lulus and learns to write a letter / Cari Best ;
pictures by Giselle Potter. — 1st ed.
     p.   cm.
  Summary: Beatrice enjoys learning to spell, and gets really
excited about it after some encouragement from her grandmother,
but she has trouble convincing her classmates that spelling is not
boring.
  ISBN 978-0-374-39904-7 (hardcover)
  [1. English language—Spelling—Fiction.   2. Schools—Fiction.
3. Show-and-tell presentations—Fiction.]   I. Potter, Giselle, ill.
II. Title.
PZ7.B46579Be 2013
[E]—dc23
                                                    2012015337

This book is not affiliated with, or endorsed or sponsored by,
the owners of the Scrabble brand name.

Farrar Straus Giroux Books for Young Readers may be purchased for business or
promotional use. For information on bulk purchases please contact Macmillan
Corporate and Premium Sales Department at (800) 221-7945 x5442 or by email
at specialmarkets@macmillan.com.

I n the beginning, Beatrice wrote letters. Not the kind of letters that start with "Dear Somebody." Letters like A B C T E R I E.

"These letters are my name," said Beatrice proudly.

"You mean those letters are *in* your name," said her brother, Leo.

"But they don't *spell* your name," said her sister, June.

"You have to put the letters in the proper order for them to spell your name," said her mother.

"Like this," said her father. "B-E-A-T-R-I-C-E."

So Beatrice tried again. And again. And again.
Sometimes she mixed up the letters that went in the
middle. Sometimes she left out the pesky E at the end.
Sometimes she forgot to put a capital B at the beginning.

"I wish my name was something simple like Bat or Cat
or even Rat," she said, trying and trying and trying to spell
Beatrice.

Then one day she did. It was at the beach. "Wahoo!" shouted Beatrice. "I can't wait to spell every single word in the world."

But unfortunately, no one in her family cared a crumb about spelling. Leo had his ant farm, June had gymnastics, and her parents had their music. So Beatrice had to wait . . .

Barikuda

Locamotive

Spegetty

. . . until her grandma Nanny Hannah came for a visit. She had no trouble answering all of Beatrice's how-do-you-spell questions one after another: "B–A–R–R–A–C–U–D–A, L–O–C–O–M–O–T–I–V–E, S–P–A–G–H–E–T–T–I."

"I wish I could do that," said Beatrice.

"You could!" said Nanny Hannah. Then she explained how.

"Like this?" Beatrice asked, taking a deep breath. She stared at the word *kindergarten* on her book bag. Then she closed her eyes, waiting to see a picture of the word in her mind's eye. A whole minute went by before Beatrice jumped up. "K–I–N–D–E–R–G–A–R–T–E–N," she spelled without a single mistake.

"You are my spelling Bea," said Nanny Hannah. "*Kindergarten* is a lulu of a word to spell."

After that, Beatrice went on a spelling spree.

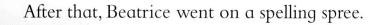

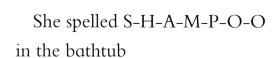

She spelled S-H-A-M-P-O-O
in the bathtub

and C-E-R-E-A-L in the kitchen,

E-M-E-R-G-E-N-C-Y on the
school bus

and S-P-I-D-E-R to her pet tarantula, Ros

The more she spelled, the more she learned the way words were put together. Soon Beatrice was sounding them out:

BA NA NA.

She noticed that, like her name, a lot of words have E's at the end that have no sound:

HOUSE,

REPTILE,

and TOOTHPASTE.

The next time Nanny Hannah came over, she gave Beatrice a present.

"No good speller should ever be without her own dictionary," she said. "Ask Thomas Jefferson."

"Who's Thomas Jefferson?" Beatrice wanted to know.

"He was the third president of the United States, the writer of the Declaration of Independence, and a crackerjack speller," said Nanny Hannah. "He told his daughter to turn to her dictionary before she ever spelled a word wrong."

Beatrice turned to *her* dictionary that very afternoon when she and Nanny Hannah played Scrabble. She made big words by combining small ones: SKYSCRAPER, MOTORCYCLE, SIDEWALK.

"That's my spelling Bea!" said Nanny Hannah. "And don't be afraid to make mistakes. That's the way good spellers learn."

With time, Beatrice got to be such a good speller that she could spot mistakes all over her neighborhood. She corrected each one.

At the pet store:
SAIL on Snakes became
SALE on Snakes.

At Lombardi's Bakery:
Fresh ZUCCINI Bread became
Fresh ZUCCHINI Bread.

At the Boys and Girls Club:
SWIMING Tonight at 6 became
SWIMMING Tonight at 6.

And at school, the ATTENDENCE chart became the
ATTENDANCE chart.

"Whoops!" said her teacher, Mrs. Blondell.

Beatrice smiled. "Spelling is my favorite sport," she said.

Beatrice loved to spell so much that she tried to get her friends interested in a spelling club. But no one signed up.

"Spelling makes me yawn," said Stewart.

"I feel like a robot when we spell in class," said Rachel. "All we do is memorize."

"I agree," said Samantha. "Let's tell Mrs. Blondell we're going on strike."

"*No more spelling!*" said Ben, followed by Brian, Amy, and Edgar.

Beatrice was crushed when her plan for a spelling club fizzled.

She called Nanny Hannah after school to tell her what happened. Nanny Hannah said, "Life without spelling would be A–W–F–U–L."

"Tell me about it," said Beatrice.

Later that night Beatrice asked Rose, "How could there be no spelling? How would we read if everything was spelled every which way?"

RASBERRY
CHEESECAKE

For the first time, Beatrice found herself in a spelling slump.
All weekend she walked past street signs without trying to
spell them. She didn't look on maps or menus for good words
to spell. She didn't even notice when Mr. Lombardi made a
lulu of a mistake in his bakery window.

Sunday night Beatrice tossed and turned.

"What would Thomas Jefferson do?" she asked herself over and over. Then she sat up. *Turn to his dictionary. That's what!*

Beatrice picked up hers and started flipping through the pages. She found herself in the T's.

"There's *tarantula*," she said, showing Rose, "and *terrarium* and *Thomas*."

Then Beatrice got a lulu of an idea.

On Monday morning, when it was her turn for show-and-tell, Beatrice stood up and walked to the front of the room. First she changed the show-and-tell sign to read SHOW-AND-SPELL.

Then she began: "This is my T-A-R-A-N-T-U-L-A, Rose, and this is her T-E-R-R-A-R-I-U-M. Some tarantulas have E-I-G-H-T eyes and some don't E-A-T for two years, but not Rose. She loves to eat L-I-V-E crickets. If Rose was poisonous, she wouldn't be my P-E-T. Any questions?"

Beatrice looked around the room. No one moved a muscle—not even to yawn. Then Stewart's hand shot up. "How do you spell *poisonous*?" he asked. "And can we see her eat a live cricket?"

"P–O–I–S–O–N–O–U–S," spelled Beatrice. Then she fed Rose a cricket.

"Rose is so C-O-O-L," said Brian.

"I have a B-O-A at home," said Edgar. "His name is Newt."

"I have four F-I-S-H," said Amy.

Everyone wanted to get in on the act—the spelling act.

"Bravo, Beatrice!" said Mrs. Blondell.

So that's how Show-and-Spell got started, swept through Beatrice's classroom, and took the entire school by storm— one word at a time.

"I have a map of the Grand C-A-N-Y-O-N," said Samantha, who likes maps. "I went there last Y-E-A-R."

"Look at this wrapper I got from a M-E-G-A M-I-S-S-I-L-E ice pop!" said Rachel. "Another word for *missile* is R-O-C-K-E-T."

"This E-G-G belonged to a real, live ostrich," said Ben. "Ostriches can't F-L-Y."

Even Mrs. Blondell brought something for Show-and-Spell.
"These are my toe shoes," she said. "They make me feel like a
B-A-L-L-E-R-I-N-A."

"*Ballerina* is a lulu of a word to spell," said Beatrice.

It didn't take long for Beatrice's friends to catch the spelling bug, too. They could be seen all over town looking for good words to spell—and for people's mistakes.

At the end of the year, Beatrice finally learned to write a letter. The kind that starts with "Dear Somebody." This is what she wrote:

Dear Nanny Hannah,

Some people get hazel eyes or chocolate chip brownies or orange sweaters from their grandmas. Thank you for giving me spelling.

> Love sincerely,
> Your Spelling Bea
> (*Sincerely* is a lulu of a word to spell.)

P.S. Do you think Thomas Jefferson got spelling from *his* grandma, too?

A a   B b

F f   G g   H h

Ll   M m

Q q   R r   S s

V v   W w